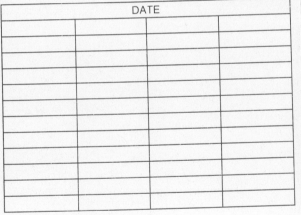

E
LOV   Love, Pamela.

             Lighthouse seeds.

                              000045141
$15.95   08/15/2005

DATE			

1899

Text © 2004 by Pamela Love
Illustrations © 2004 by Linda Warner

Cover and interior design by Lindy Gifford

Printed in China

6   5   4   3   2   1

ISBN 0-89272-541-9

Library of Congress Control Number 2004101630

DOWN EAST BOOKS
Camden, Maine
a division of Down East Enterprise, publishers of *Down East* magazine

For catalog information and book orders, visit
www.downeastbooks.com or call 800-685-7962

Lighthouse
Seeds

By Pamela Love
Illustrated by Linda Warner

Down East Books
Camden, Maine

To all those who garden under difficult circumstances,
especially Sally Love, Andrew Love, and Arthea Kammerer
—P.L.

To my mother, for teaching me the joys of reading,
creating art, and growing a garden
—L.W.

"There it is," Mother said, pointing. "Our new house."

Sarah shivered. She told herself it was because of Maine's March wind, not the sight of the lighthouse on that lonely rock in the sea. "It's like a desert," she said.

"A desert?" her brother, Tom, snorted. "Look at all the water!"

Look at it? Sarah *felt* it spraying her face and shoving the boat up and down. This far offshore, the ocean seemed alive. "I meant, there aren't any plants," she said.

"The island is so low that the sea has scrubbed off any soil. Nothing can grow there." Mother sighed. Sarah knew how much her mother loved gardening.

But that was when Father had kept a lighthouse on the coast. Now, he'd been assigned to one on a rock ledge miles from anywhere. Without its lighthouse, boats could crash onto the rock in the darkness of night or during storms. So this place would be Sarah's home for years. Once again, she shivered.

Her braids whipping wildly in the wind as she stepped onto the dock, Sarah helped carry in food and other supplies. There'd be no trips to the store from here.

Once, Sarah stumbled, dropping a little box. Small colored envelopes spilled out and started blowing away.

"No!" Mother cried, snatching one out of the air. Tom grabbed another, and Sarah threw herself onto the dock, saving the rest.

Panting, Sarah asked, "What are they?"

Mother took a deep breath. "Our seeds. Oh, I know there's no way to grow things here. But someday, somewhere, we will have another garden. Maybe we'll start it with these seeds."

Time passed. Each day, after reading and arithmetic lessons with Mother, Sarah and Tom helped Father care for the lighthouse beacon. They spent many hours cleaning its glass. "Any dirt could keep sailors from seeing the light," Father explained.

Sometimes fishermen brought supplies out to the ledge. The family looked forward to these visits. "Nothing's better than company, even with the extra cooking," Mother declared.

When the weather grew warmer, Sarah and Tom could go outside. They collected shells and looked for boats. Bird watching was fun too—sometimes gulls would feed from their fingertips. Best of all were the times when Father showed them how to row the dory.

"Watch your step," Mother warned them whenever they went outside. Holes and cracks covered the rock, many of them the right size to catch a foot. The closest doctor was days away.

Soon Sarah and Tom knew that ledge as well as their names. Then one day, Sarah spotted a dandelion.

"Never thought I'd be happy to see a weed," said Sarah, surprised. "However did it get here?" Kneeling, she saw that the dandelion was growing in a little clump of soil.

"The seed must've been in the mud from a fisherman's boot," Mother said at dinner. But when Sarah eagerly suggested they make a garden, Mother shook her head. "With nowhere to lay it out? No soil? And waves to wash away any that was brought in?" Suddenly, she stood, yanking dishes from the table. Sarah wasn't done eating, but something in her mother's face made her hurry to help.

As she cleared the rest of the dishes, Sarah watched her mother from the corner of her eye. Mother's mouth was a thin, firm line— she never smiled now.

In fact, Mother almost never left the lighthouse. She didn't complain, but Sarah knew how unhappy she was living there.

While making her bed the next morning, Sarah ran her fingers over the tulip design on her quilt. "Except for that dandelion, these are the only flowers on the island."

"How can I help Mother?" Sarah asked herself, then set her jaw. "She wants a garden. If a dandelion can bloom here, so can more flowers—with help." Coming up with a plan would take time, but she had plenty of that.

Sarah's uncle was a fisherman. On his next visit, Sarah took him aside and asked a favor. Laughing, he said he would bring what she wanted.

When he returned, Sarah hid the sack he'd delivered in the boathouse. That night, she sneaked outside. She didn't tell anyone what she was doing because she didn't want her mother to be disappointed if the plan didn't work. The moon and the beacon gave Sarah enough light. Dragging the sack of soil along, she crammed handfuls of dirt into any hole or crack that might protect it. Whispering a prayer, Sarah sprinkled seeds from her pocket—some of the ones Mother had brought with her.

Finally, the soil and seeds ran out. Sarah hid the sack again, then washed off her hands in the sea.

Just as Sarah reached the door, it opened suddenly. Sarah had never seen her mother so angry. "What were you doing?" she demanded. Before Sarah could explain, Mother snapped, "Never mind. There's no excuse for your being outside at night without telling someone! You know how dangerous it is.

"You'll stay inside for the next week and not go on the next boat trip to the mainland. Now go to bed."

For the next several days it rained. Sarah didn't dare ask her
brother or father to check on the flowers. She was afraid they'd
think she had been foolish. When the storm ended, no one
mentioned seeing the makeshift flowerpots she had fashioned in
the rock. "Those seeds are fish food now, most likely," Sarah
thought sadly.

Finally Sarah was allowed out. Hoping that at least one plant
had survived, she explored the ledge. To her surprise, tiny patch-
es of green had sprouted all over!

Now Sarah told her family what she had done.

"You put those mud puddles there? I thought they came from the sea!" Tom exclaimed.

Mother pressed her face against the window. Her broom clattered to the floor as she banged the door open. Sarah watched her bend down, gently touching one flower after another. When she returned to the porch, her face was wet—but not from sea spray. She squeezed Sarah's hand.

From that day on, Mother and Sarah often came outside to check on the flowers' progress. Weeks later, orange nasturtiums, red zinnias, and blue bachelor's buttons stuck out of the ledge almost everywhere. "Never thought I'd see this place bloom," Father said.

One stormy night, there was a crunching sound outside.
Some fishermen were tying up their leaking boat to the dock.
While they dried off, Sarah and her mother fed them hot soup.
"Thank you kindly," said the captain between spoonfuls.
"Not just for the hospitality. For the flowers."

"The flowers?" Sarah asked.

He nodded. "We spend weeks at sea, fishing. Nothing's around but sky and water. Seeing flowers out here . . . Well, your light-house garden reminds us that we have homes to go back to."

In her heart, Sarah felt a glow as strong as the lighthouse's.

Author's Note

This book is based on a true story.

During the 1800s and early 1900s, the lighthouse keepers and their families who lived on Mount Desert Rock, twenty-six miles off the Maine coast, raised flowers (and vegetables) in the way described here. Local fishermen called the ledge "God's rock garden." Of course, harsh winter weather meant that everything had to be replanted each spring.

The lighthouse on Mount Desert Rock is now maintained by the United States Coast Guard.